Captain Blownaparte and the Golden Skeleton
Part Three

by Helga Hopkins
Illustrated by David Benham

First published as an eBook in 2017
Paperback edition published in 2018

contact@blownaparte.com

ISBN-13: 978-1720777779
ISBN-10: 1720777772

Captain Blownaparte™
and the Golden Skeleton

by Helga Hopkins & David Benham

Part Three: Dodgy the Octopus

Part 3 - Dodgy the Octopus

Captain Blownaparte and his crew were having a well earned rest after their last adventure with the sea serpent. The Captain was polishing gold coins - his absolute favourite hobby. Sproggie, the Captain's little nephew, was on deck playing football with the ship's crew. Prosper, the clever parrot, and the golden skeleton were discussing where they could find the rest of the skeleton's bones. Suddenly, they were all interrupted by Pirate Tidy, who'd been out doing some shopping.

'You'll never guess what I've just seen!' he puffed, completely out of breath. 'Captain Purplebeard and his crew have just turned up in The Pirates Tavern.' Captain Purplebeard as we all know is Captain Blownaparte's arch enemy, and they've fought many battles against each other in the past. 'And that's not all,' spluttered Pirate Tidy, 'Purplebeard is wearing a necklace made from golden bones!' 'What!' screeched the golden skeleton, 'Those bones belong to me!'

'Well, he's not going to give 'em up willingly,' sighed Captain Blownaparte. 'OK, so how's this for a plan,' said Swiss Sepp. 'Let's make a huge stink bomb from my smelliest Swiss cheese! Sproggie can smuggle it into the tavern and in seconds all the pirates will pass out from the cheese fumes and we can grab the golden bones.'

'Hold on, I don't want to pass out in The Pirates Tavern.' grumbled Sproggie. 'You won't need to' said Sepp. 'You'll only be carrying the wrapped up cheese into the tavern, and Turnip the rat will unwrap it. The fumes won't affect him at all – rats love smelly cheese!' So Sepp prepared the smelliest cheese he's ever made in his life and wrapped it up in a neat parcel.

Sproggie, Captain Blownaparte and Turnip made their way to The Pirates Tavern, with the Captain being the only one brave enough to carry the cheese. Both Sproggie and the Captain wore pegs on their noses to make sure the awful smell wouldn't affect them.

When they reached the tavern, they peeped through the window, and saw the place was full of the nastiest pirates they'd ever seen. And the nastiest of them all, Captain Purplebeard, was sitting right in the middle of the tavern surrounded by his extremely nasty crew. Sproggie took the cheese from the Captain and sneaked into the tavern with Turnip. He quickly hid the cheese under Captain Purplebeard's table and rushed outside again.

Now it was Turnip's turn. The fearless rat unwrapped the cheese and released the deadly fumes. Within moments, all the pirates passed out and instantly fell into a deep cheesy coma. Turnip scampered onto the table and lifted up Captain Purplebeard's eyelids to make sure he was well and truly asleep. Then, a thumbs up from Turnip signalled the waiting Captain into the tavern to unravel the golden bones from Captain Purplebeard's neck.

The golden skeleton was highly delighted to have his long lost back bones back in place! In the meantime Prosper, the clever parrot, had discovered the whereabouts of the skeleton's other arm bones. It seems that Dodgy, the legendary card playing octopus was using the arm to rake up his winnings. 'Oh dear,' grumbled Alfredo, 'we'll have no chance; Dodgy always wins because he cheats, but nobody knows how he does it!' 'I know,' said Prosper proudly, 'he mixes the cards so quickly with his tentacles, no one can see him hiding the winning cards in his hat band.'

'I've got an interesting idea,' giggled Turnip. 'My rat friends could pinch the good cards from Dodgy's hat band and exchange them for losing cards! My special friends Spike and Woody would be good; I don't have the figure for those kinds of gymnastics!' So they decided that Pedro would gamble with Dodgy, and the rats would swap the cards to make sure Pedro would win.

Soon Pedro was sitting opposite Dodgy waiting for the game to start. But Dodgy was very suspicious of Pedro and his friends. 'Oh my dear, he's going to notice the rats at this rate,' worried Captain Blownaparte.

'We'll have to turn his attention to something else,' said a steely eyed Prosper. 'Dodgy adores fish cocktails, so we'll send Sproggie to make some up at the table. 'What are fish cocktails made up with?' asked Sproggie. 'Fish innards and fish tails gently stirred in ginger beer topped by a generous dollop of hot mustard.' said Prosper. Sproggie's face turned green, but he bravely put the peg on his nose again and grumbled quietly, 'I get all the smelly jobs me!'

Dodgy started to mix the cards. He did it so fast you could barely see them, and all the while one of his tentacles was stuffing the winning cards into his hat band. But just as swiftly, Spike and Woody grabbed the winning cards and exchanged them with Pedro's losing cards – and Dodgy didn't notice a thing.

Then, when Pedro won the game, Dodgy angrily bellowed that he must be a cheat! 'It takes one to know one,' gurgled Captain Blownaparte as he grabbed the golden arm and raked all the winnings toward Pedro.

Dodgy huffed and took off in a cloud of dark blue ink. His hat, with some left over playing cards still stuck in the hat band, gently floated after him.

Back on ship, the golden skeleton couldn't believe his luck when he got his second arm back. 'The only thing missing now are the golden legs.' said Sproggie. 'But I hope our next adventure is going to be a lot less smelly!' Everybody collapsed laughing as they tucked into an extra large dinner – but on this occasion, cheese was not on the menu!

PEDRO ROSIE CAPTAIN
BLOWNAPARTE

PROSPER

SPROGGIE

SPIKE

TURNIP

PIRATE TIDY ALFREDO SWISS SEPP

Manufactured by Amazon.ca
Bolton, ON

21789901R00021